PHILIPPE DUPASQUIER

PAUL'S PRESENT

W

It was the first day of term in the New Year.

Everyone in Paul's class was talking about what they got for Christmas.
"I got some rollerskates," said Jenny.

“You should see how fast I can go on my new skateboard,” said Mark.

"I got a transformer, which becomes a spaceship!" exclaimed Kevin.

Stanislas said he had been given a *real* telescope. "I can see the stars," he said.

The twins had been given a set of walkie-talkies so they could keep in touch . . .

. . . and Arthur had terrified all the
the neighbours with his Dracula fancy dress costume.

Although everybody had fantastic presents they all fancied Dimitri's set of drums with four cymbals and a gong. Of course, Christopher Smart had something special . . .

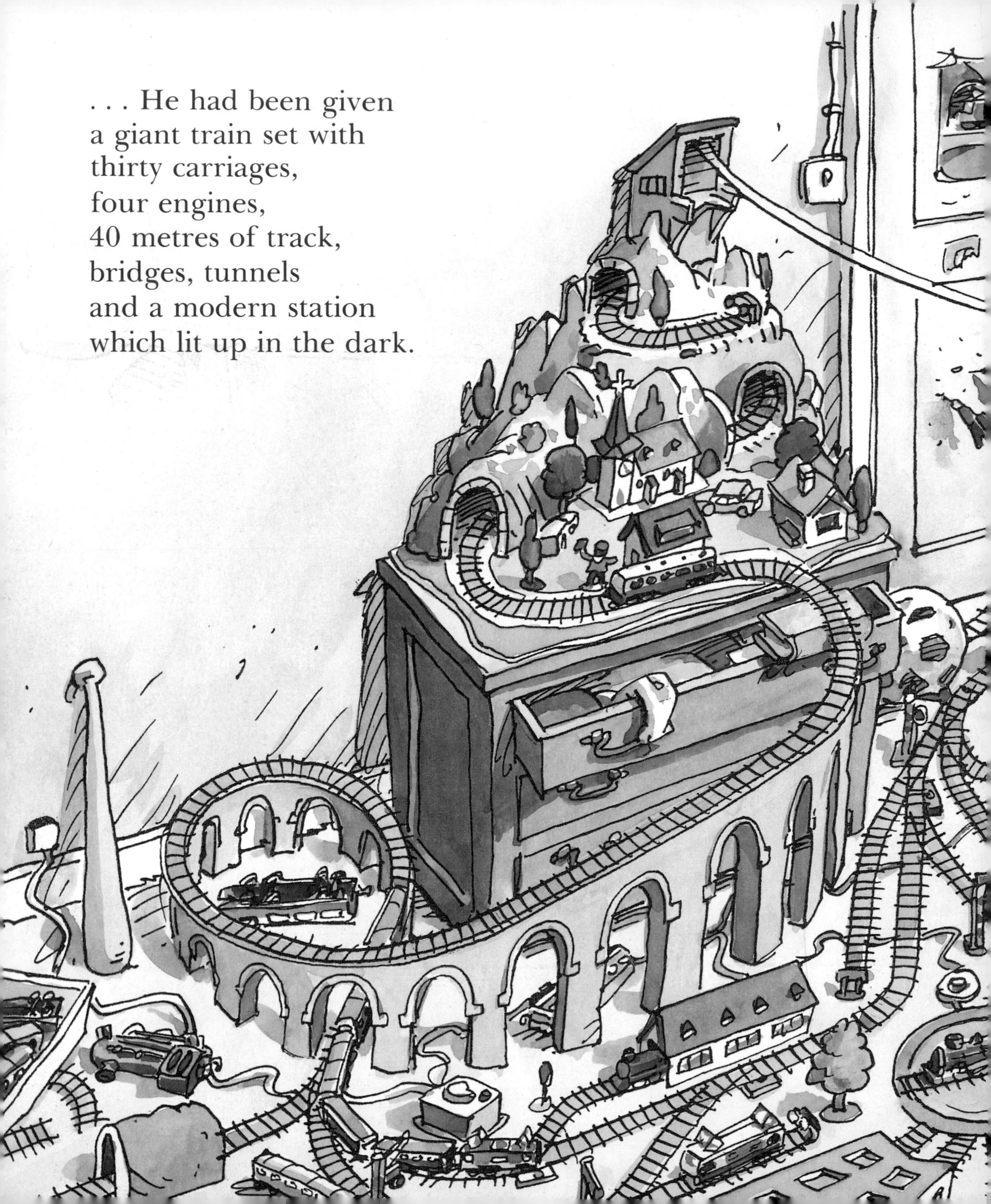

. . . He had been given
a giant train set with
thirty carriages,
four engines,
40 metres of track,
bridges, tunnels
and a modern station
which lit up in the dark.

Trust him to have the best present of all.
"And what did you get for Christmas, Paul?"
asked Jenny.
"Yes, what did you get, Paul?" asked all his friends.

Paul had been given a hamster and he had brought him to show everyone.

He showed off the hamster's little house, exercise wheel and special drinking container. Everyone wanted a go at holding him.

When he escaped they all joined in chasing him around the classroom. "I wish I had a hamster," said Nikita.

"Yes, it's the best present of all," said Lorraine, and even Christopher agreed.

"Next year I'm going to ask for a goldfish," said Lorraine.

"I want a parrot," said Oliver, "to play pirates with."

Arthur said he wanted a bat,
to complete his Dracula outfit and scare his baby sitter.

"I want a camel to carry me to school," said Nikita.

"Oh! I want a pig," exclaimed Babette, "to eat up my school dinner."

Corina thought it would be good to have a whole flock of sheep to help her get to sleep, but Christopher Smart, of course had to have something special . . .

. . . He wanted a safari park with dolphins, flamingoes and a collection of the rarest butterflies in the world. There would also be six fierce lions to frighten off unwanted visitors.

"And what will you ask for next year, Paul?" asked Jenny.
"Yes, what will you ask for Paul?" asked all his friends.
"Oh! I'm going to ask for the same thing I asked for this year," said Paul.
"What? Another hamster," chorused everybody.
"Of course not," said Paul. "What I always wanted is . . .

. . . a speedboat!"

First published in Great Britain 1992
by Andersen Press Ltd
Published 1994 by Mammoth
an imprint of Reed Consumer Books Ltd
Michelin House, 81 Fulham Road, London SW3 6RB
and Auckland, Melbourne, Singapore and Toronto

ISBN 0 7497 1377 1

A CIP catalogue record for this title
is available from the British Library

Printed in Great Britain
by Scotprint Ltd, Musselburgh